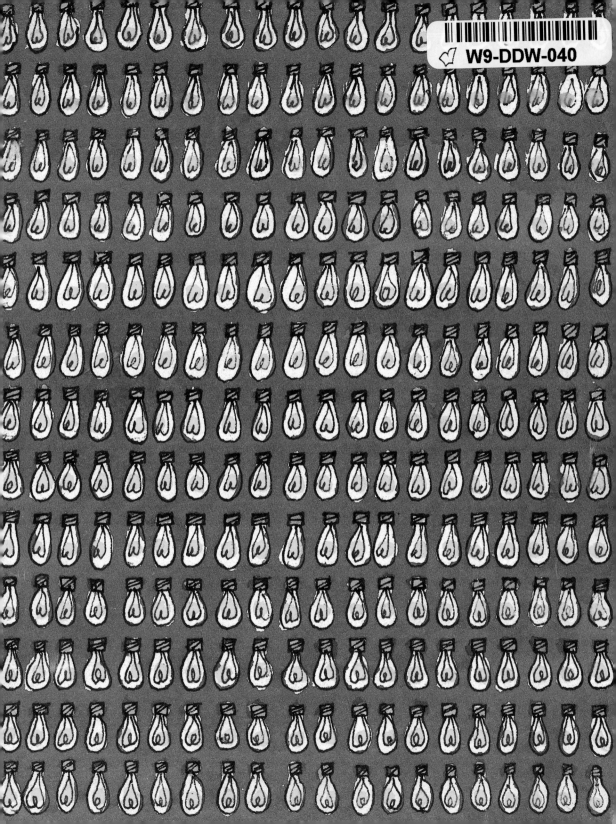

W9-DDW-040

FUNNY BUNNIES ON THE RUN

by Robert Quackenbush

CLARION BOOKS

New York

NORTHPORT PUBLIC LIBRARY
NORTHPORT, NEW YORK

For Piet, Margie,
the Haas Family,
and Putty

Clarion Books
a Houghton Mifflin Company imprint
52 Vanderbilt Avenue, New York, NY 10017
Text and Illustrations © 1989 by Robert Quackenbush

All rights reserved
For information about permission to reproduce
selections from this book, write to Permissions,
Houghton Mifflin Company, 2 Park Street,
Boston, MA 02108
Printed in the U.S.A.

Library of Congress Cataloging-in-Publication Data
Quackenbush, Robert M.
    Funny bunnies on the run / Robert Quackenbush.
        p. cm.
    Summary: When the lights go out at home, the Bunny Family flips
every switch with no success until the power returns and the bunnies
find themselves in trouble when all the appliances go on at once.
    ISBN 0-89919-771-X
    [1. Rabbits—Fiction.   2. Electric apparatus and appliances—
—Fiction.]   I. Title.
PZ7.Q16Fv 1989
[E]—dc 19   88-20361   CIP
                                                        AC

Jacuzzi is a registered trademark of
Jacuzzi Whirlpool Bath, Inc.

Y 10 9 8 7 6 5 4 3 2 1

Mama and Papa Bunny
and little Lucy Bunny
hurried to finish dressing.
It was going to be
a wonderful evening!
They were giving their
biggest party ever, and
the first guests would be
arriving at any moment.
Suddenly…

...the lights went out!
Papa Bunny got flashlights.
"Try all the switches,"
he said. "See if
anything goes on."
The Bunnies ran around
the house turning on the
lights and machinery.
Nothing worked.
"Oh, no!" wailed Mama
Bunny. "Just when guests
are coming!"

All at once the lights
went back on.
At the same time
a terrible roar
came from all directions.
Every machine in the house
had been switched on
when the lights went out!
"Shut off the stereo!"
yelled Papa Bunny.
That done, they heard
a racket coming from
the kitchen.

"Quick!" said Mama Bunny
in horror. "I left something
in the blender!"
They raced to the kitchen,
but were stopped at the door
by flying raspberries
for the party punch.

Papa Bunny grabbed a lid
for a shield to protect
himself.
He made it to the blender
and shut it off.
Then they all saw water
dripping from the ceiling.

"The Jacuzzi is overflowing!"
cried Mama Bunny. "I must
have turned it on when
I was trying switches!"
They tore upstairs.

They stopped the water
from pouring out of the Jacuzzi.
"Whew!" they said.
Then they heard *churn, churn,*
click, click, churn, churn
coming from the den.
"My computer is printing!"
said Papa Bunny.

They rushed to the den
and waded through
a sea of printouts
and shut off the computer.

They all flopped down
on the sofa.
"Oh, let me catch my
breath," sighed Mama Bunny.
Then the Bunnies heard
whirl, whirl, whoosh, whoosh
coming from downstairs.
"The fan over the
party table!" said little Lucy.
"It's going at high speed!"

Down to the party table
they sped.
They saw napkins, paper plates,
party favors, and streamers
all whirling around.
They fought through the mess
and shut off the fan.
Then they heard
splash, splash, grind, grind.
"Oh, no!" they cried.
"The washer and dryer are on!"

They galloped to the laundry room.
Soap suds were oozing
out of the washer.
The dryer was going at
such a speed that it was
thumping along the floor
and knocking things down.
No sooner had they shut off
these machines when they heard
"Help! Help!" coming from
Grandpa's room.

They pounded back up the stairs
to Grandpa Bunny's room.
There they found him
being knocked about
by his mechanical bed.
They shut it off as
quickly as they could.
Fortunately, Grandpa Bunny
was not hurt.

At last all the machines
in the house were shut off.
Mama, Papa and little Lucy
trooped downstairs.
"I never knew we had so
many machines," Mama Bunny said.
"Why do we?" asked Lucy Bunny.
"I've forgotten," said Papa Bunny.
Just then the doorbell rang:
Ding! Dong!

The first party guests had arrived.
They looked at the wreckage
and at their hosts' wilted state.
"Goodness!" they said....

"Is the party over already?"